ISBNs
979-8-9867664-2-3 (paperback)
979-8-9867664-1-6 (ebook)

ENDS OF JUSTICE

WALKING ON BROKEN GLASS
LIFE AFTER DOBBS
POSTER CHILD
SAFETY FIRST

SARA PARETSKY

SARA & 2 C-DOGS PRESS

WALKING ON BROKEN GLASS

A hot June night, New York, 1970. I started calling hospitals, looking for my roommate. I learned she'd been picked up on 117th Street, unconscious from blood loss, and taken to the ER at Columbia-Presbyterian, where they'd done an emergency D & C. In the morning, when she had recovered enough strength to be discharged, the male resident told her she was trash, a welfare queen who hadn't deserved to have her life saved.

She'd been scared, leaving the apartment, and so she'd confided in me: she was pregnant, the man involved was married and a high-ranking city official who wanted no part of her now she was pregnant. New York had legalized abortion that year but the first clinics weren't up and running yet and she couldn't afford to give up a chance at a spot in Columbia's journalism school.

I offered to go with her, but she preferred to go alone. I was her roommate, not a friend, but a stranger who'd answered an ad. I was white, she was black, and she had no reason to believe I could understand the many ways race affected her decisions. (And of course I couldn't.)

Her near death sent me back to Chicago that fall as a passionate abortion rights advocate, lobbying to overturn Illinois's anti-abortion laws.

I can still remember the day that Roe was handed down, the sense of a burden being lifted, a sense of freedom.

That sense was short-lived as the National Council of Catholic Bishops and other groups revved up opposition to women's healthcare. I became a clinic escort, helping women pass through mobs that screamed obscenities at us. They kicked us, spat on us, even once bit one of my sibling escorts, circled me screaming, "Christ killer, baby killer," drove a car onto one clinic's sidewalk to run over a security guard.

I wrote op-ed pieces, I chaired the board of the National Abortion Rights Action League of Illinois, I spoke at fundraisers, I marched, I tried to persuade newspapers to cover the vile behavior of anti-abortion zealots.

After a million people gathered on the mall in Washington in 2004 for the march for women's lives, the *New York Times* gave a two page spread to the anti's who'd shown up. They photographed them looking soulful, praying the rosary. They didn't photograph the obscenities or the kicking and biting.

Over a fifty-year span, media covered almost none of the 862,000 acts of violent hate against clinics, patients and providers. This violence included murdering abortion providers and threatening to kill children of other providers[1].

------

1 Details available at the National Abortion Federation website

On June 24, 2022, when the supreme court announced the death of Roe, I looked back on my 50 years of action and felt as though I had had my own innermost parts cut out. I feel today as I did in the weeks after my husband's death. I wake up every morning and the Constitution is still in tatters, and American women are still treated like chattel animals.

I also wake up every day determined to fight back by all means within my power. My main power is speech, the spoken word, the written word.

In 1982, I published the first novel in my series about a Chicago private eye. V.I. Warshawski is physically tough, but her true fearlessness lies in her speech. She says those things that those with power want to keep silent, hidden, out of public discourse. V.I.'s speech hits home, as I can tell from the hate mail I receive.

V.I. grew up under the shadow of Chicago's former steel mills. At their peak, operating three shifts, those mills employed forty thousand people. Skies were yellow at midnight from the sulfur fumes, but families could own their own small homes and buy a new car every few years. Now that neighborhood is in ruins, with more vacant lots than houses, forty percent unemployment, and gang shootings a relentless reality.

At a library reading I once gave, ten women stayed behind after everyone else left. They told me they were married to unemployed steel workers; they worked three jobs to keep food on the table and to stay ahead of mortgage payments.

They hadn't read a book since high school, they said, until someone told them there was a novel set in their homes. They had bought hardcover copies of the book on their meager incomes. They wanted them signed.

"V.I. gives us courage to play this hard hand life dealt us," one woman said.

I think of these women almost every day, and most especially now, as women's rights to speech, to make our own healthcare decisions is being outlawed.

"Nevertheless, she persisted," was Mitch McConnell's patronizing explanation for why he shut up Elizabeth Warren for questioning Jeff Sessions' qualifications to be Attorney General.

It was an arrogant remark, but he was also bewildered. He'd told a woman she couldn't speak, but she kept on talking.

One of the seminarians who attacked patients when I was a clinic escort told me he was there "to make sure these girls have help in living their lives right."

His statement—"to make sure girls have help in living their lives right"—and the youth's concomitant harassment of our patients, are a clear residue of the many millennia that treated women as male property. This seminarian, who was himself so young he wasn't yet shaving, did not see women going into a clinic, he saw girls.

Unconsciously—or not so unconsciously—many Americans still think of women as girls, as children unable to make decisions about their own lives. This view so pervades our own culture that many educated, otherwise empathic people cannot understand why women object to being called girls.

Think seriously about this word for a minute. A girl is a child. Most cultures, in most times, have viewed women not as full, legal adults but as a cross between children and chattel animals.

The first measures of the Taliban government were directed against women. They were denied access to schools, confined to the home, allowed outside only with a male relative, beaten if they showed their hands or ankles outside their blinding burkhas. All this was done in the name of protecting women's "virtue." Which really means, controlling women's sexuality. Just as our nation's highest court, and many of our state legislatures are doing today.

Little girls, courts and legislatures are telling females of all ages, I am your daddy, I know what's best for you, and you must have my permission for what you do with your bodies, whether in your bedrooms or at your doctor's office. You must, as one of George W. Bush's top health advisors, Dr. William Archer, told his Texas patients who sought contraceptives or abortions, "bend to my will."

On July 27, 2022, five weeks after Dobbs, a twelve-year-old girl confronted the West Virginia legislature as they rushed to outlaw abortion. "If a man decides that I'm an object and does unspeakable and tragic things to me, am I, a child, supposed to birth and carry another child? Am

I to put my body through the physical trauma of pregnancy? Am I to suffer the mental implications, a child who had no say in what was being done with my body?"

She added, "Some here say they are pro-life. What about my life? Does my life not matter to you?"[2]

The answer was no. The legislature voted 69 to 23 against her life and that of all other West Virginia women and girls.

In 1992, the *Chicago Tribune* published an attack on me and Sisters in Crime, the advocacy organization for women crime writers I helped create. The reporter claimed my goal was to get rid of books by men. To underscore how dangerous I was, he attacked my appearance—I was "ominously" dressed all in black; I had "a pointed nose and eyes that cut and slash." I sounded like a cross between the stereotype of the predatory Jew in Protocols of the Elders of Zion and the Wicked Witch of the West. All because I advocated for women's speech to be recognized on a par with men's.

And yet, I have persisted. As has Elizabeth Warren. And the women of South Chicago. And Shannon Brewer, the fierce and fearless director of the Pink House, the Mississippi clinic which she ran for the poor women of Mississippi, until the Supremes in Dobbs forced her to close.

---

2. Although newspapers reported the girl's name, I am withholding it out of respect for her privacy as a minor.

As the Japanese poet Yosano Akiko wrote in 1910:

> The day when the mountain will move is coming.
> In antiquity, mountains, all aflame, moved about.
> (No one need believe this)
> But, all of you, believe this:
> All the women who have been asleep
> Have now awakened and are on the move.

This is the legacy I want to leave for my time on this planet: that we women are awake, we are on the move. We will not tolerate the death and destruction of the lives of women and girls. We will not tolerate another season of silence. We will persist.

LIFE AFTER DOBBS

Spared the flames
I returned to Domremy
Minded my brothers' children and their sheep
Seasons came and went
My hair changed from burnished copper to duller bronze
and then to grey
Cataracts grew across my eyes
And children sidestepped the hero of Orleans –
Not that old woman with her threadbare fables of lead-
ing troops to war!
Each spring new lambs arrived
I sang them lullabies
Recounting those old battles
Where freedom triumphed

And in the greater world the citadel collapsed
The king whom she'd adored gave up their victories.
Word came to her, not St. Michael, nor St. Margaret
Word came from girls violated beyond their bearing

And so, old though I am, cloudy eyes hunting through cupboards and chests,
Yes, there is my armor, rusted from disuse
My stiff knees protest, my back jolts me with pain
But I bend my bones to my will
Pulling on the greaves
Arthritic fingers struggle with buckles and vambraces
My old horse hears the clang of shield on steel
Whinnies in a creaky voice
Stands as I find a stool,
Climb up
One tired old leg over the pommel
And so once more to battle

POSTER CHILD

The fog was thick along the lakefront that morning. Through the ghostly layers of cotton, the man looked like a drunk who had passed out in a gush of his own vomit—not something passersby wanted to get close to.

It wasn't until a woman tried to yank her dog away from the pile of litter around the bench that anyone knew the man was dead. He'd been hit in the face hard enough to destroy his eyes, and what was coming from his mouth wasn't vomit, but a wad of anti-abortion fliers, sticking out so that it looked as though he was eating a dismembered child.

The woman's legs gave way. She wanted to scream but she couldn't make a sound. The dog stood in the middle of the lake path, barking madly, and a cyclist, going too fast in the fog, collided with it and fell over in a heap of bike, grass and goose shit. He started upbraiding the woman, but she pointed dumbly at the bench; the cyclist finally called 911, but yelled at the woman for not controlling her dog while he righted his bike and took off again into the fog.

The woman thought she heard a child crying, but her legs were too unsteady for her to investigate. After a moment, she decided it was just a gull screaming.

Larry Pacheco took the 911 call because he was already near the scene. The baby killers were holding a fundraiser on a boat anchored near Randolph Street. This had brought abortion opponents out in force to protest. Some lined Lake Shore Drive, holding up posters that showed slaughtered babies. Another group heckled people attending the fundraiser as they got out of cars and taxis near the mouth of the harbor.

Pacheco was one of some half dozen officers assigned to make sure protestors and baby killers didn't get physical with each other. How any woman could kill her own helpless little baby while it was inside her, Pacheco couldn't understand for one minute. When he found out his older sister had had an abortion, he'd beaten her so hard he'd had to take her to the emergency room afterward, to get her eye and her lip attended to. But she needed to understand, murder was murder, and if the law wouldn't punish her, she still had to face the consequences.

Even so, something about these baby savers, lovers, whatever they were, Pacheco couldn't explain it, but they didn't seem quite right to him, either. What kind of job was it for a grown man, like this Arnold Culver—forty-seven years old, eight children—was that a real job, going around the country attacking doctors, holding up posters covered with bloody body parts?

The fundraiser had been going for a couple of hours when Pacheco got the 911 call. His legs hurt from standing around the harbor mouth for hours. He plodded slowly through the cold, damp air to the body.

Like the woman with the dog, Pacheco blenched at the fliers dribbling from the dead man's mouth, but he texted his sergeant, told what he'd found: murdered man, probably blunt force trauma, send for detectives.

If Lieutenant Finchley, the Area Six watch commander, had realized how high-profile the victim would prove to be, he would have summoned an experienced pair of detectives from the field. When the desk sergeant relayed Pacheco's message, though, the report sounded as though the victim were a homeless man. Finchley sent the two detectives who were in the squad room, Oliver Billings, who Finchley thought was lazy, and Billings's partner, rookie detective Liz Marchek.

At the lakefront, Billings and Marchek found the body easily, despite the fog: at least five patrol cars were flashing their blue-and-whites near the Monroe Street intersection. When one patrol sees something interesting, most nearby units join in, partly to protect their buddies, in case a situation turns ugly, partly for something to do.

Oliver, sticking a hand into the victim's jacket pockets, found the wallet with his ID. Arnold Culver.

"Culver?" Pacheco blurted. "I just saw him outside the harbor where the baby killers are meeting. He had a bunch of kids, and some lady attacked him there, but he was alive."

"Baby killers?" Liz asked. "We've got baby killers meeting openly on the lakefront and we're just letting them go about their business?"

"He means abortionists, rookie," Oliver said. "Some kind of fundraiser—the boss mentioned it at roll call."

Liz batted her eyes at her partner. "Thanks, Ollie, the technical language confuses me sometimes."

The evidence team joined them, and Liz went back to the body with them. "Blows look like they came from above," one of the techs said. "The ME may be able to say how tall the assailant was, but looks like anyone could have done it—they wouldn't have to be big, just damned angry."

Anyone who followed the abortion controversy in America knew that Culver had made plenty of people angry. Depending on your perspective he was either an innovator in ways to stop abortions, or a perverse maniac who didn't respect boundaries of person or property. At any time he faced dozens of lawsuits, but he also had the deep pockets of the nation's anti-abortion churches behind him, so he continued to do things like drop explosives from helicopters onto freestanding clinics, stalk the children of clinic workers, or egg his followers into shooting doctors.

Liz went back to her partner, who was stepping Pacheco through the attack on Culver he'd witnessed earlier.

The mist had been so heavy earlier that you could hardly see cars until they were on top of you, Pacheco said. "Me and Mueller, we were standing outside the harbor, and suddenly one of those holes opened in the fog, and I saw Culver. He had four kids with him, two maybe were teenagers, the other two seven, eight, something like that."

Culver had been handing fliers to the kids; Pacheco said he looked as though he was also giving them instructions. When a white-haired woman in a dark raincoat got out of a cab, Culver sent one of the smaller children toward her with a flier.

Over the noise of traffic and water, Pacheco couldn't hear what the woman said. "But she was plenty mad, detective, the way she moved—she grabbed the paper, rolled it up, threw it at Culver as hard as she could."

"Doesn't sound like much of an attack," Liz objected. "He hit her or anything?"

"The fog covered them up. I walked over, to see if they needed, you know, separating, but the woman was already on the gangway to the boat."

Culver had vanished in the mist with two of the children; the other two, one of the teens with one of the little ones, remained at the mouth of the drive with a stack of fliers. Every time a car stopped, they chanted in shrill unison, "Thank you for not murdering us!"

Pacheco told Oliver he was pretty sure he'd know the lady if he saw her, so they walked on up to the yacht. The last speech was just ending when they got into the dining room.

The cops circled the room and Pacheco found the woman sitting near the podium. Liz recognized her at once: Dr. Nina Adari, who performed abortions at a Loop clinic.

Dr. Adari was so stunned when Oliver and Pacheco bent over her, asking what she knew about Arnie Culver, that she didn't look at Liz.

"What do I know about him? He's a bully and a thug. Why? Has he attacked someone?"

"Other way around, ma'am," Oliver said. "We need to ask you a few questions about the fight you had with him this morning."

"Fight?" Adari repeated as if it were a foreign word she'd never heard. "I don't fight with people. If Culver is claiming that, then you can be sure he's lying."

"Not what we heard, ma'am. We heard you were the last person seen with him. And that you attacked him."

"Do you mean he's dead?" Adari said sharply.

"Why would you think that?" Oliver said.

"Has he disappeared then? I certainly did not attack him. He used one of his children to hand me a disgusting flier, which I threw in Arnie's face, but I don't think that constitutes an attack. Not compared to his assaults on my clinic and on my staff, which the police have paid no attention to."

One of Adari's tablemates put a hand on the doctor's arm. "Take it easy, Nina. Wait until you know what they want before you tell them what you know."

The buzz started through the dining room at once—Arnie, Jr. was dead. He'd been murdered. He'd been run over by a car. No, the police had found him floating in the harbor. It was amazing how fast a room full of people could turn a single fact into a labyrinth of conspiracy. Liz heard someone at a nearby table ask, with a nervous snigger, how late-term was a forty-seven-year-old abortion?

When the people near Adari realized the police were taking her with them, they crowded around her, protesting about Adari's rights, and her innocence.

"She's not under arrest, just coming with us to answer some questions, right, ma'am?" Oliver said.

The group pulled back, murmuring uncertainly. One advantage to picking up older white women at fundraisers instead of gangbangers in drug houses, Liz thought—they and their friends weren't usually combative. On the other hand, the room was lousy with lawyers, and three of them, a man and two women, were at Adari's side when the cops walked from the room with her.

"Are you charging her?" one of the women lawyers asked.

Liz squinted to read her name badge: Leydon Ashford. Only the hyper-privileged walk around with two last names. Liz tried not to get her hackles up, but she really did not want some snot of a lawyer in the interrogation room with her.

"Not right now. We want to talk to her," Oliver answered, his easy smile in place. He used his smile like a cook with a sugar sifter, knowing just how much he needed to sweeten the pastry.

The three lawyers rode down the escalator with Adari and the cops. They all offered to come to the station with her.

"She doesn't need a lawyer," Liz said. "We just want to ask her a few questions."

"Everyone needs an attorney," Leydon Ashford responded. "I'll ride over with you, Nina. See that they dot all their 'i's' and so on."

The crowds began to gather outside the station long before the detectives arrived with their "person of interest." Adults with rosaries and angry signs—*Abort the Baby Murderers; Stop America's Holocaust/Protect the Unborn* and the ubiquitous blow-ups of bloody body parts—were kneeling on the walks right up to the edge of the driveway. They'd brought children with them, children who should be in school, Liz thought, not camped in front of a police station to hear their parents scream curses at a squad car.

"Drive around to the back," Oliver said. "We don't want them attacking the car."

Liz drove past the front gates without slowing. "What are they thinking, involving their children in something like this? This isn't a TV set."

"Yes, it is," Oliver Billings peered in the wing mirror as Liz whipped around the corner. "The camera crews are setting up."

Liz called the desk sergeant on her radio to let him know they were coming in through the back. "You know there's a crowd out front, don't you, Tommy? Oliver says the networks are all there. He says the Christian Broadcast truck was behind us on Roosevelt Road."

"Been watching them on the monitor," the desk sergeant said. "If I'd wanted to work in a circus I'd a learned how to swing from a trapeze. I'll let the looey know you're here."

When the detectives reached the back of the station,

fog shrouded the heads of the protestors kneeling by the rear gates, making them look like guillotined corpses.

The protestors didn't try to block the car when the desk sergeant released the gates, but they pounded on the windows and spat as Liz drove past.

"If these are the Christians, the lions don't stand a chance," she muttered to Oliver.

"Their leader's dead; they're angry," he said. "And they know we've got a suspect in the car."

When they finally got through the back entrance and into Lieutenant Finchley's office, the lawyer who'd ridden over with Adari asked Finchley how the abortion foes knew the cops were bringing the doctor in for questioning. "Did you tell them that Dr. Adari was coming to the station?"

"Nothing we do is very secret," Finchley said. "People listen in to police scanners, they video our cops coming and going and put it on the Net. You know that as well as I do, ma'am. And you and Dr. Adari also know how high tempers are going to be riding over Mr. Culver's death, so let's try to keep the rhetoric at a manageable temperature, okay?"

Finchley had a uniformed officer escort Adari and the lawyer to an interview room before pulling Liz and Oliver into his office. "Okay, you two, everything you know. Now. Why did you bring the doctor in?"

"Pacheco—the uniform who found Culver's body—he saw her assault Culver outside the boat where the fundraiser was taking place," Oliver said.

"How'd he know who it was? He study this abortion rights group?" Finchley said.

"No, sir," Liz explained why Pacheco had ID'd Dr. Adari. "We looked up her history online—he's been harassing her, she's got a couple of lawsuits against him personally and against his organization."

"Even so," Finchley said, "she's not very big, and she must be twenty years older than Culver on top of it. It's hard to believe she could have attacked him, let alone killed him."

"Element of surprise in the fog, Looey," Oliver suggested. "And whoever killed him was furious—dude had been hit on the head so many times the eye-sockets were destroyed."

Finchley grunted. "Any priors on the Adari woman?"

Oliver hunched a shoulder. "Not since her student days. She dates back to the Vietnam war, got arrested three times in the seventies, once for pouring blood over an Army recruiter."

"Marchek—anything more recent than thirty years ago?"

Liz saw the pulse throbbing in Finchley's left temple. "Uh, well, sir, she seemed to be investigating Culver, trying to dig up some kind of dirt on him, maybe, to stop him targeting her clinic."

"She find anything?"

"We'll ask her that when we talk to her, sir."

"You two need to tread very carefully here. The cardinal has already been on the phone to me, as has the mayor, and the head of the local ACLU, and I can guarantee that Fox and CNN are going to keep this on a 24-hour loop. Any suspects you talk to, especially here at the station, you follow regs down to the smallest subparagraph. *Capisce?*"

"Yes, sir," Liz said.

"And if either of you talk to the press, even to a ten-year-old blogger, you will be walking night patrol in South Chicago for the rest of your short lives."

"Yes, sir," Liz repeated.

"Yazzuh, boss." Oliver sketched a salute.

The lieutenant frowned, which sent Oliver grumbling into the interview room. Every time Finchley refused to laugh and joke with Oliver Billings, the detective magnified the size of his grievance against the new commander. The fact that Finchley was black and Billings was white only made the relationship more volatile.

Liz pretended sympathy with her partner's complaints about Finchley, because Oliver had proved more than once that he'd blindside her in the field if he thought she wasn't supporting him.

Privately, she was glad the old commander had left. She'd only served under him for two months, but he used jokes as a thin cover over his efforts to put women officers off-balance. When he'd assigned her to Oliver, he'd eyed her with a leer and told Oliver to "shape her up, not that there's anything wrong with the shape she's already in." The late-night, post-shift drinking sessions with his special cronies not only created divisions in the station, but brought his buddies, including Oliver Billings, to work with chronic hangovers.

She and Oliver stopped outside the interview room for a word with the officer who'd been listening to the hidden mikes. Leydon Ashford apparently suspected the police could eavesdrop—the officer said the Dr. Adari and her lawyer had murmured so softly into each other's ears that he hadn't picked up anything.

Oliver pulled a chair away from the table and leaned back in it, legs crossed: the suspect was supposed to be lulled into thinking it was a casual chat. He announced his and Liz's names for the recording equipment, but before he could launch into his first question, the doctor narrowed her eyes at Liz.

"Have we met, detective?"

"I don't think so, ma'am, unless I was on patrol for an event like today's." Liz's tone was wooden.

Oliver cleared his throat, demanding attention. "I understand you and Arnie Culver had a history, doctor."

"Every abortion provider in this country has a history with Mr. Culver. Recently, most doctors who prescribe contraceptives have started having a history with him." Dr. Adari had her hands folded in her lap.

"Is that why you attacked Culver outside the fundraiser this morning?" Oliver asked.

"I can't add to what I told you earlier," the doctor said. "He used one of his children to hand me a flier. I tossed it at him. Is that an attack? Is it similar to the time he lit gasoline-soaked rags and threw them at me?"

"That's what we want to know, doctor," Oliver said. "Did you follow him down the lake path? Have a confrontation that got out of hand?"

"No. I told him not to abuse the children he brought into the world by forcing them into his private anti-abortion army, and then I went into the fundraiser, where any number of people can tell you I spent the entire lunch hour. Is there anything else you want to ask me? I have patients waiting."

"To abort their babies?" Oliver asked.

The doctor said, "My patients' privacy is sacrosanct, detective. I can't tell you why they consult me. I can only tell you that it's unprofessional of me to make them wait."

The lawyer said, "Right. If you have any further questions for Dr. Adari, you can call me." Ashford put one of her business cards on the interview table. She nodded at Adari and the two women stood.

"What about the private eye you hired to investigate Culver?" Liz asked.

"What about it, indeed?" the lawyer said.

"How did he react to the investigation?" Liz persisted.

"I expect someone in his organization could tell you," Adari said.

"He was suing you for invasion of privacy," Oliver said, "so we can assume he wasn't happy about it."

"He knew a lot about invasion of privacy," Adari said.

The lawyer took her firmly by the arm and steered her from the room.

"Good of you to join in the interrogation there at the end," Oliver said to Liz when the women had left. "I thought you'd turned into a deaf-mute on me."

Liz smiled. "I'm the rookie, remember? I'm learning from you."

"You're the bigmouth licking Finchley's ass. Why don't you use your tongue on Culver's kids. It'll give you practice for when you have some of the little darlings yourself."

"And what will you be doing while I'm honing my day-care skills?" Liz demanded.

"Dr. Adari hired someone to investigate Culver. That's worth investigating."

Liz rented the third floor of a converted workman's cottage on the city's northwest side, but when she finished interviewing the Culver children, she headed to her grandfather's apartment in Rogers Park, near the lake.

After her mother was killed in a botched police raid when Liz was nine, her grandparents had raised Liz and her brother Elliot. Grandma Judith had been dead for some years now and Grandpapa lived alone in their old apartment. Even though he'd retired from Temple Etz Chaim, he was still the wisest man Liz knew.

She hadn't always felt that way. As a teenager, she'd battled with him furiously over her mother. She had fought with Elliot, who said their mother was asking for trouble by being part of an anarchist cell, and with Grandpapa, who, she said, sided with the police against the poor. She announced she was an anarchist who didn't believe in God, hoping to spark rage in Grandpapa, but he only reacted by calling her "My little anarchist," when he gave her his blessing.

When she told him she wanted to join the police, he'd been troubled, and asked her pointed questions about her motives. "Do you imagine yourself as some kind of resistance hero, infiltrating the police so you can read their covert files?"

It was their last serious argument, because she didn't want to admit how close he was to the truth. Grandpapa hadn't believed she could be a happy cop, but she'd actually taken to the work. Five years on patrol and then she'd passed the exam to become a detective.

"Detective Anarchist!" Grandfather greeted her when she arrived this evening. "Still keeping order in an uncontrollable world?"

He didn't follow the news; he hadn't heard about Culver's death and she didn't tell him, just asked about his arthritis, about Mrs. Gelinsky and Mrs. Mannheim, who were competing for his attention, and about the cat, Bathsheba, who ruled the house in the absence of a human female.

"You hear from your brother?"

"Every day, Grandpapa. If you would learn to text, you'd hear from him, too." Her brother Elliot was in Denmark, testing and repairing computer security at his firm's Copenhagen headquarters.

She went into the kitchen to make supper, knowing her grandfather wouldn't have bothered to cook a meal just for himself.

"And what's troubling you, little Anarchist," he asked when she'd put an omelet in front of him.

"Nothing. Why can't I stop by to make you supper just because I love you?"

He smiled. "I'm grateful, even if you're telling only a portion of the truth."

"Omitting the truth, Grandpapa. How big a sin is that?"

He nodded: she had revealed the real reason for her visit. "The rabbis put a great deal of thought into that, and the answer is—it all depends. If you're protecting someone from harm, versus trying not to embarrass yourself, versus trying not to show off, versus not violating your own privacy--I would need much more information before I could give you an answer. Did you omit the truth in talking to someone? Or did you commit *g'neivat daat*—theft of the mind—encourage someone to believe a falsehood?"

His omelet grew cold as he talked. By the end of the evening, Liz thought if she believed in God she'd be in even worse trouble than she was already, but she didn't say it out loud. Not that she had to—Grandpapa realized that when he put his hands on her forehead to bless her, before she left him to drive to her own place.

Whether God was angry with her, Liz couldn't say, but Lieutenant Finchley definitely was. When she arrived at Area Six the next morning, there was a note taped to the desk she shared with two other detectives: Marchek, see me ASAP. Cops usually texted each other; a written note was ominous.

The lieutenant sent the desk sergeant away and shut his door. "Why didn't you tell me as soon as you brought Adari into the station yesterday, Marchek?"

Liz stood with her hands clasped behind her, feet apart, as if she were at inspection. The pulse above the lieutenant's left eye was throbbing, a danger sign.

"I'm taking you off this case."

"But, sir—"

"There is no 'but, sir,' in this conversation. The victim photographed you going into the suspect's clinic. How did you expect to keep that a secret?"

"I didn't think my medical history was anyone's public business, sir. Not the victim's, and not my co-workers."

"Your medical history is your business, Marchek, which is why I'm not posting this on the World Wide Web, but when any officer in my command has had prior contact with a suspect or a victim in an investigation, I hear about it first from that officer, not from someone in the Evidence Unit sifting through the victim's papers, unless you think you are V.I. Warshawski, able to operate outside standard systems with impunity. If we don't come up with a better lead in the next forty-eight hours, you and every patient Culver ever photographed will be a person of interest in this crime. Do I make myself clear?"

"Yes, sir." Liz dug her fingernails into her palms to keep her voice from shaking.

"You will assist Sergeant Wrexall at the front desk and catch up on your paperwork backlog until I decide you're ready for the street again. Send Detective Billings in to see me when he arrives. You're dismissed."

Liz wanted to know what the lieutenant was going to say to Oliver, but his manner was too forbidding for her to ask. She kept her head up, her shoulders back, as she walked to the front desk. G'neivat daat, theft of the mind, wasn't in the Illinois Criminal Code, but Lieutenant Finchley knew the punishment for it, anyway.

Fortunately, Sergeant Wrexall acted as though it was an ordinary event, detectives to be put on desk duty.

At nine-thirty, when her partner arrived, Wrexall said, "Billings, the looey wants to see you. Whatever you do, don't complain about hemorrhoids—he decided mine were hurting my job performance so he took your partner to help me out here."

After five minutes with Finchley, Billings stalked to

the front desk, his lips thin. "What did you tell Finchley about our investigation?"

"Nothing. He called me in this morning and told me I was riding a desk for now—what did you tell him about me?"

"That you're a useless rookie. He's putting Clevenger and Cormack in charge of Culver and asking me to assist—to be a third wheel! I was this close to handing in my badge."

Oliver held out his thumb and forefinger a quarter inch apart and Liz and Wrexall nodded sympathetically. Oliver's father, two uncles and grandfather had all been Chicago cops. He would never resign. Liz felt a flood of gratitude to the lieutenant wash through her. He'd protected her privacy; he hadn't outed her to Oliver Billings.

"Who is V.I. Warshawski, anyway?" she asked Wrexall when they were alone again. "The looey asked if I thought I was like her."

"She's a P I. Gets on a lot of cops nerves because she takes risks and cuts corners we can't—and also because she has an annoying habit of popping up in high-profile cases and solving them."

"Maybe she'll pop up and solve Culver's death," Liz suggested.

Thirty-six hours passed with no viable leads, and no sign that V.I. Warshawski was going to pop up. In twelve hours, Lieutenant Finchley would turn the photographs from the Evidence Unit over to the investigating detectives. Liz would become a person of interest—one among however many thousand Culver had photographed at abortion clinics, but the one whose private history would become part of her partner's arsenal when he wanted to tear her down. Maybe even end her police career just as it was getting going.

If Liz had known Culver was taking her picture when she went into Adari's clinic, she might have killed him on the spot. If the looey hadn't threatened to make her private business public, Liz would have been happy to see Culver's murderer walk free, even if the Sixth Commandment didn't give you the option to choose who you did or didn't murder.

When Wrexall's shift ended, Finchley was still in the station. Liz went to her own desk, pretending to busy herself with cold-case files. Liz kept on working through the shift change. Finchley finally left for the day, with a grunt at Liz to let her know she was still on probation, but holding up well. Liz waited until she was sure the lieutenant had pulled out of the parking lot before going over to Oliver's desk and logging on to his computer. She could have accessed the Culver case from her own machine but she didn't want a trail following behind her.

Culver's password was easy—his badge number plus the jersey numbers of his two favorite athletes. Liz loaded the case notes onto a flash drive, logged off, and was in her car before third shift roll call started.

She drove to an Internet cafe in one of the busy student neighborhoods. She even paid to park—no point in some meter maid reading her plates and noting that a cop had parked here. I'm a thief, she imagined herself telling Grandpapa, a thief of information who knows my guilt so thoroughly I'm trying to hide my tracks in someone else's computer. Even as she squirmed, she paid cash for time on a machine.

The Culver murder was important enough that plenty of people had written notes into the case file. The report from the crime lab: Culver had been killed by one of the sticks used in the posters the protestors had carried along Lake Shore Drive. Someone searching the crime scene had found the shattered pieces of wood covered with Culver's brains and blood, but they hadn't found usable prints or any DNA besides the victim's.

Oliver had entered his notes on the investigation Dr. Adari had started into Culver's life and finances. Adari hadn't discovered anything criminal, although Culver had been taking home close to a million dollars a year from his organization. Oliver had written, "Major motive here," in the margin. Liz shook her head—that was a motive for Culver to kill Adari, not the other way around.

She trolled through blogs and social networks for a bit—sometimes killers made coy comments on websites, eager for recognition of how clever they'd been. The anti-abortion vitriol was so extreme across the Net--directed at Dr. Adari, who deserved to be in everyone's gun sights, according to many posts--that Liz stopped reading it.

She did find a number of photos of Culver, taken at the protest by his adoring supporters, and now posted as precious icons of his martyrdom. Some of the shots showed him with the four children who'd accompanied him to the march. The two boys were dressed in identical pale-blue blazers and ties, the girls in frilly white dresses with blue ribbons, despite the chilly weather.

When Liz had gone to the house two days ago, before Finchley took her off the case, the girls still had on the frilly dresses they'd worn to the march and the younger boy, Jimmy, was wearing his pale blue blazer and a tie. Only the oldest boy had shed his formal clothes for a sweatshirt and jeans. Maybe that was the one place where he could vent a rebellious adolescent spirit. Liz thought of all her teenaged fights with Grandpapa—maybe it would have been better if her only rebellion had been to wear a sweatshirt to Temple.

The Culver house had been spilling over with children—Arnie's eight, augmented by a dozen more belonging to the neighbors and in-laws who'd gathered to console the widow.

Liz had mouthed the conventional phrases to Culver's widow: sorry to disturb you, but if I could talk to the children who were with your husband this morning? She tried not to flinch from the crucifixes on the walls.

"I thought you'd made an arrest," one of the neighbors said. "One of the baby killers."

Liz shook her head. "We're just gathering information. That's why anything the kids saw or heard could help."

The women reluctantly brought forward the four who'd been with Arnie. Lucy, the oldest of Culver's eight children, seventeen, followed by Paul, sixteen, and Veronica and Jimmy, seven and eight.

"We take turns going with Dad," Lucy said, when Liz asked why they'd been at the fundraiser with Arnie. "It was Paul's and my turn, and we're training the little ones, how to talk to ladies when they're about to go into death chambers, how to tell them not to kill their unborn babies." Her voice was soft, matter-of-fact.

"Your teachers are okay with you missing school?" Liz asked.

"We're home-schooled, so the atheists can't force us to deny Christ crucified the way they do in school."

The words seemed to be spoken by rote, auto-pilot. Liz wondered why the parents didn't send the children to Catholic school—there were more than enough to choose from—but she knew she shouldn't get into an argument with the children, or the mother.

"So two of you stayed at the harbor to hand out literature, and two of you went with your dad?"

"Jimmy and I, we were at the harbor. Paul and Nicki—Veronica—they went on down the path with Daddy. Daddy was checking on the pickets—our people get discouraged sometimes standing all alone. You can't believe the horrid things Christ haters shout out of their cars. One of our ladies was even crying. Nicki cheered her up, didn't you?"

The eight-year-old nodded without speaking. Paul and Jimmy were silent, too. When Liz asked what they'd seen or heard on the lake path, they just shook their heads.

"The lady you gave the flier to, the one who threw it at your daddy, did you see her on the lake path?"

Nicki and Paul shook their heads again.

"Were you together the whole time?" Liz asked idly.

Nicki gasped, as if Liz had guessed a secret, but Lucy said, "Of course they were together the whole time."

"I thought you stayed up by the yacht where the fund-raiser was," Liz said. "What did you see, Nicki?"

"I didn't see, I couldn't see, there was a fog," the younger girl said, breathlessly. "I thought I lost Paul but he was right next to me the whole time. I started to cry, I mean, I almost started to cry."

"That's right. You're a big girl and only babies cry," Lucy said.

Liz tried to probe, gently, sure she'd seen something that frightened her, but Lucy kept answering for her sister, until one of the adults said the children had been through enough. No more questions.

Now, in the Internet cafe, Liz tried to think it through. The child had seen something, but what? Had she run away from her brother, the way children do—geese, seagulls, boats, all more interesting than one more abortion protest in a life that had clearly been filled with them—and been scolded? Or had she seen her father's assailant?

It was eleven p.m. now. Liz tried to fight down her panic. Think, think, there's a clue in here some place. Her own notes—the woman who'd discovered the body had said she thought she heard a child crying.

That had probably been Nicki. The little Culver girl who thought she'd lost her brother in the fog. She'd started to cry when she was supposed to be cheerful. What an abominable way to treat a small child!

Panic, and now anger. Two bad companions for a detective. Liz unplugged the flash drive and went back into the night.

She drove to the crime scene, but it was too dark to

see anything. Liz's brother owned an apartment down-town; he'd given Liz a key when he left for Denmark. She crossed the park and let herself in, slept a few hours in his guest bed, but as soon as the sky began to lighten, she went back to the bench where Culver's body had been found.

The wind had shifted in the night; the fog that had shrouded the city for the last week was finally gone. Liz paced restlessly around the lakefront and the harbor. The benches were filled with the homeless, their possessions carefully laid beneath them to avoid midnight predators. Liz checked each man she came to for a sign of life, but she didn't try to waken them, not until she'd covered a quarter of a mile and found one of them with a pale blue jacket folded under his head.

Finchley himself drove out to La Grange with his detectives and the jacket. He let Liz join the team, but told her she was still on probation; she was not to say anything.

When Mrs. Culver came to the door, Finchley showed her the jacket. "We think your son, Paul, lost this in all the confusion on Monday, ma'am, but we want to make sure it's his before we send it to the lab for tests."

In the background, he could hear the children, the oldest girl, Lucy, explaining an arithmetic problem to a small child just out of his sight; a Spanish lesson streaming over the Internet in a corner of the living room. The children were so used to adults coming and going at all hours that they didn't pay attention to the police, until Nicki, passing by with a peanut butter sandwich, shouted,

"Paul, they got your jacket."

The doorway was suddenly filled with children; as in *Peter Pan*, they seemed to tumble from every doorway, every piece of furniture. Mrs. Culver looked around her in bewilderment.

"Paul, is this your jacket? Did you lose it at the protest on Monday?"

The boy's face turned very white. He stared at it for a minute without speaking, then his face contorted into sobs.

His mother frowned at him. "We don't cry in public, Paul, we control ourselves for the sake of Jesus, who died for us without crying."

"I'm tired of Jesus!" Paul shouted.

His brothers and sisters gave a collective gasp and shrank from him.

"I don't want to be a show child, I don't want to be in court so everyone can see you had a million children and never used birth control, I don't want to go to marches and clinics, I want to play football and have a life like other guys my age! I told you this a million times, I told Dad, but neither of you ever gave a damn about any of us! We were just props to you, props you could show off in public. He sat there on that bench starting to lecture me on my duty to the unborn and I said, 'what about your duty to the born, to us, your children,' and he hit me! He hit me one time too many.

"I picked up that sign, that stupid picture of all those bleeding babies. He worshipped those bleeding babies but it didn't matter how many times he made us bleed! And you, you just said, amen, praise Jesus to whatever he said, so I hit him, I wanted him to see how it felt, and I just kept hitting him and hitting him and hitting him, and then Nicki started to cry because there was blood on my jacket. So I dropped it in the harbor and took her for an ice cream, and the rest of you can go kneel down and say your rosaries but my only prayer is, 'thank God that bully can't hit any of us again.'"

Back at the station, Liz asked Finchley what would happen to Paul.

"He's still a minor. There's a lot of psychological stress. If they get him a good lawyer he might have a chance."

"Whoa, that mother!" Billings said. "She'll skin him and fry him herself if the state doesn't do it."

"Yeah, that was my impression, too," Finchley agreed. "Marchek—what were you doing at the crime scene this morning, when I'd given you a direct order to stay away from the case."

"Uh, sir, I couldn't sleep, I was taking a walk." What did Torah say about an incomplete truth that resulted in a lie? Liz couldn't remember.

"Marchek, if I was Mrs. Culver, I'd hand you over for disciplinary action. I'm even less merciful than she is—I'm putting you back on the street with Billings. But if you ever again have private contact with a witness to a crime, whether you run into them sleep-walking or meet them in your synagogue, you tell me about it first. Or you give me your badge. Got it?"

"Yes, sir." Liz saluted and left the room.

"What was that about?" Oliver demanded.

"I was showing off," she said to Oliver. "He didn't like it."

G'neivat daat, that was it. Theft of the mind. She'd just told another half-truth. Maybe quarter truth. She'd tell Grandpapa the whole story tonight and see whether he thought the rabbis gave her any wiggle room.

Poster Child *was originally published in* **Send My Love and a Molotov Cocktail,** *Gary Phillips and Andrea Gibbons, eds. PM Press, 2011.*

She guessed cameras, or at least microphones, were hidden in the cell. Possibly in the showers, the cafeteria, even the attorneys' meeting rooms. From the moment of her arrest until the day of the trial, she said nothing inside the prison, except immediately after her arrest, and that was only to repeat a demand for a phone call. Finally, when she'd been kept sleepless and could no longer be sure of time, a guard handed her a cell phone and told her she had thirty seconds, and if she didn't know the number, they weren't a phone directory, so tough luck.

Once she'd made the call, she became mute. She didn't speak to the assistant attorneys for the Northern District of Illinois sent to interrogate her, nor to the guards who summoned her for roll call four times a day, or tried to chat with her during the exercise period. Because she was a high-risk prisoner, she was kept segregated from the general population. A guard was always with her, and always tried to get her to speak.

The other women yelled at her across the wire fence that separated her from them during recreation, not rude, just curious: "Why are you here, Grandma? You kill your old man? You hold up a bank?"

One day the guards brought a woman into her cell, a prisoner with an advanced pregnancy. "You're a baby doctor, right? This woman is bleeding, she says she's in pain, says she needs to go to the hospital. You can examine her, see if she's telling the truth or casting shade."

A pregnant woman, bleeding, that wasn't so rare, could mean anything, but brought to her cell, not to the infirmary? That could mean an invitation to a charge of abuse, malpractice. She stared at the pregnant woman's face, saw fear in her face and something less appetizing, greed, or maybe unwholesome anticipation. She sat cross-legged on her bunk, closed her eyes, hands clasped in her lap.

The guard smacked her face, hard enough to knock her backward. "You think you're better than her, you're too good to touch her? Didn't you swear an oath to take care of sick people when they gave you your telescope?"

In the beginning, she had corrected such ludicrous mistakes in her head. Now, she carefully withdrew herself from even a mental engagement: arguing a point in your head meant you were tempted to argue it out loud.

She sat back up, eyes still shut, took a deep breath in, a slow breath out. Chose a poem from her interior library. German rhymes from her early childhood: *Über allen Gipfeln ist Ruh*. English poems from her years in London schools: *Does the road wind uphill all the way*?

When her lawyer finally arrived, three weeks after her arrest, she still didn't speak inside the small room set aside for attorney-client meetings. The lawyer explained that it had taken them that long to discover where the doctor was being held. "They're fighting very dirty," the lawyer said.

The doctor nodded. *Come back with an erasable board,* she wrote on an edge of the lawyer's legal pad. When the lawyer had read the message, the doctor tore off the handwritten scrap and swallowed it.

She was being held without bond because she was considered a flight risk, the lawyer explained. "We tried to fight for bail, but these new Homeland Security Courts have more power than ordinary federal courts. We are challenging the Constitutionality of both your arrest and your post-arrest treatment. We have our own investigators tracking down information and witnesses in your support. Keep heart: there are hundreds of thousands of people in America and across the world who are aware of your arrest and are protesting it."

After the lawyer left, the guards took the doctor to a new cell, one with three other inmates. Those women were noisy. One had a small radio she played at top volume at all hours. Another heard voices telling her to pray or scream or, on their third day together, to attack the doctor. The radio player was shocked into calling for a guard. When no one came, the radio player grabbed the woman hearing voices; the fourth cellmate joined her. Together they subdued the voice-hearer.

"You gotta file a complaint," the radio player said. "You can't let people be trying to kill you. That's what they want, you know, they told us they hoping you'll die, or that we'd annoy you so much, you'd attack one of us. They didn't say you was an old lady who wouldn't hurt a flea. So you gotta file a complaint."

The doctor almost touched the radio player's shoulder, remembered in time that a touch could be turned into a sexual caress by clever camera editing and clasped her hands in front of her. The following day, she was back in her old cell, one bed, just her, alone.

After that, she was sent to exercise with the general population. The woman who'd attacked her tried to do so again, joined by several others who liked to prey on the old or friendless – including the woman who'd been brought to her with a problem pregnancy. "She's a doctor but she only treat people with money!"

The radio player intervened. She had plenty of friends or at least followers within the prison, and she summoned enough help that the attackers withdrew.

"You a doctor?" the radio player demanded. "Why you in here?"

The doctor shook her head. Because they were outside, presumably far from microphones – although these days you probably were never far from a camera or a mike – she risked a few words.

"I don't know." Her voice was hoarse from disuse.

"How come you don't know? You know if you killed a patient, right? You know if you stole money from Medicare. So what you do?"

The doctor couldn't help laughing. "True, I'd know if I did either of those things. I didn't do them. I don't know why the United States government arrested me."

"You got some big fish pissed off," the radio player nodded sagely.

After that, people approached the doctor during exercise in the yard. The radio player served as an informal triage nurse. Swollen nodes in necks or armpits, varicose veins, heavy periods, no periods, bruises, knife wounds.

The doctor had limited ability to treat, no way to conduct a proper exam, but she would recommend the infirmary or a demand for hospital care or in most cases, wait it out – which is what the inmates would have to do in any event, even the women whose swollen abdomens didn't indicate pregnancy but ovarian tumors.

Finally, seven months and twenty-three days after her arrest and arraignment, the trial began.

The clerk of the court: "Docket number 137035, People v Charlotte R Herschel, MD, Homeland Security Court, Justice Montgomery Sessions presiding.

"Dr. Charlotte Herschel is accused of violating United States Act 312698, An Act to Guarantee the Security of the Borders of the United States, known as "The Keep America Safe Act," paragraphs 7.183 through 7.97 inclusive, relating to the medical treatment of undocumented aliens and to the willful concealment of undocumented aliens from the federal government. She is charged further with violating paragraphs 16.313 through 16.654, relating to the sanctity of the life of all United States-born citizens, from the moment of conception."

Justice Sessions: "Today's hearing is held in camera. Because the Security of Borders Act addresses Homeland Security, neither journalists nor civilian observers can be present. I must ask the bailiff to clear the courtroom of everyone but the lawyers and their assistants."

Some forty people from the Ex-Left were in the court-room. Predictably, they raised outraged howls at being ordered to leave. In fact, many of them lay limp on the floor. The bailiff and federal marshals didn't suppress grins as they banged the protestors into the benches or against the doorjamb on their way out of court.

About the only legislation the 115th Congress had passed was the Keep America Safe Act, and its follow-on, the law funding the Homeland Security courts. Dr. Herschel's case was one of the first to be heard in a Homeland court.

The law was sketchy on what defendants could do to support themselves. They could not have a trial by jury – a tribunal of five federal judges was empaneled for each trial. Defendants could call witnesses, but it wasn't clear on the presence of citizens in the courtroom. Justice Sessions had decided that matter, at least for Dr. Herschel's trial.

From the moment of her arrest, Dr. Herschel's case had been drawing attention from the Extreme Left and their fake news machines. The *New York Times* huffed and puffed so often that a Real News cartoon, showing the paper as the Big Bad Wolf unable to blow over the government's case, went viral. Of course, in response, the Ex-Left tried to paint the government as a trough full of pigs, but everyone agreed that the *Times* response was a lame knock-off of the Real News original.

However, the *Times* coverage meant that the Ex-Left fat cats put up so much money for the doctor's defense that Ruth Lebeau had agreed to take the case. Lebeau was a formidable Constitutional lawyer with a team of experienced research lawyers at her side. Except for the court reporter and Dr. Herschel, she was the only woman in Justice Sessions' courtroom, and the sole African-American. She seemed to pay no attention to that distinction, nor to the insults lobbed by Real News, comparing her to a talking chimpanzee.

Opening statement of Melvin Coulter, federal attorney for the Northern District of Illinois:

"Dr. Herschel is well known to federal agents throughout the Northern District. She runs what she calls a medical clinic, but is in reality a squalid den where the most vile crimes are committed. She not only harbors known enemies of the United States, but is a self-proclaimed murderer of the most innocent lives in our midst. So heinous are the crimes, and so intent is this so-called doctor on keeping them from public view, that she spent a small fortune in turning her abattoir into an armed fortress."

Coulter droned on for over an hour. Ruth Lebeau, dressed in navy suiting with an Elizabethan collar framing her face, made a few notes, but spent most of Coulter's speech either smiling reassuringly at her client, or mouthing comments to her chief associate, a young man whose impeccable tailoring matched her own. He seemed to find Lebeau extremely witty. The court reporter noticed that he often covered his mouth to keep from laughing out loud – a gesture which made Justice Sessions scowl with fury. The reporter was surprised that Sessions, who was known for his short fuse, hadn't expelled the lawyer from his courtroom.

Dr. Herschel was a small woman, with greying hair cut close to her head. She wore no make up and no jewelry. The court reporter thought she looked like the kind of doctor you could trust, not the formidable monster described in the government's brief. It troubled the reporter that the doctor didn't look at Coulter or Sessions during the opening statement. The reporter believed innocent people could stare down their accusers. She didn't know that sociopaths could also stare down their accusers and that innocent people might look at their clasped hands so that judge and prosecutor couldn't see the furious contempt in their eyes.

When the prosecutor sat down, Ruth Lebeau made her own opening statement. She sketched Dr. Herschel's history: an orphan, a refugee, who had dedicated her life to the health and welfare of women in the United States. The many awards she had received for her humanitarian work, for her innovations in perinatal medicine and in surgery. Lebeau spoke about the Constitution, as well, and how the law under which Dr. Herschel was charged, set up two classes of people.

"We're skating perilously close to Nuremburg laws here. Americans reject the idea that one class of person has higher value than other classes, whether the division is between black and white, Christian and Jew, foreign-born or native born. We will show that Dr. Herschel's whole life and career have been devoted to caring for women and children who most need help, and that she has used her own resources to bring free medical care to Americans who can least afford it, but need it most."

The court adjourned for lunch. Melvin Coulter was seen eating with Justice Sessions and the other judges on the tribunal. A photograph of them together in the Potawatomi Club circulated on Fake News websites, but Real News assured Americans that there was nothing wrong with two old friends meeting for lunch. The Ex-Left also put up videos of the federal marshals dragging protestors from the courtroom; Real News showed patriots cheering the marshals.

In the afternoon, the evidence part of the trial began. The government had been surveilling Dr. Herschel and her clinic for many months. Even before the Keep America Safe Act, ICE agents had paid particular attention to her Damen Avenue clinic because she treated so many low-income women, not just immigrants from Muslim countries and Mexico, but poor Americans as well.

Coulter began with photographs of the Radbuka-Herschel Family Clinic projected onto the three screens in the courtroom. These days the clinic was padlocked, the windows covered with obscene graffiti, as well as swastikas and "death camp" in jagged capital letters, but the pictures had been taken during the surveillance and data gathering phase of the case.

The clinic stood near the corner of Damen and Irving Park Road in Chicago. The sidewalks were dirty, the nearby storefronts rundown or boarded over. The court watched two women in headscarves approach the building, one with toddlers in a double stroller, the other carrying an infant while an older child held her skirt.

The women glanced around furtively, then rang the clinic bell.

"You can see the armor-plated glass." Coulter tapped the windows in the photograph, "and the video cameras. Once the women gained entrance through the first door, they were sealed in the equivalent of an airlock while clerks videoed them. Only then did they gain admittance to the death chambers inside."

The testimony of all the Immigration and Customs Enforcement Agents, along with the FBI, took close to two weeks to hear. The most dramatic testimony actually came from one of Dr. Herschel's own nurses: Amy Shazar had worn a tiny body camera to record many of Dr. Herschel's patients and procedures, even patients she herself was examining.

When Ruth Lebeau rose to cross examine her, Shazar broke down into sobs. "They threatened to deport my own mother, my sisters, back to the men who raped them. What else could I do?"

"Find someone to help you fight them," Lebeau said. "What did you think you were doing to the patients entrusted to your care?"

After Shazar's weeping went into its second inarticulate minute, Justice Sessions ruled that Lebeau was badgering the witness and to stop such an emotional line of questioning. When Shazar stepped out of the witness box, she tried to approach the doctor, but Dr. Herschel turned her head away and refused to look at her.

The court reporter didn't know how to react. If she'd been a patient in the clinic, she sure wouldn't have wanted her own private business shown in a courtroom.

But had it really been fair for the FBI to coerce Shazar into recording people? And the nurse was truly sorry – shouldn't Dr. Herschel at least accept Shazar's apology?

During Shazar's testimony, Coulter showed videos that she had taken. "Yes, Dr. Herschel routinely performed abortions in her abattoir. And she helped illegal immigrants avoid federal agents."

The five male judges, the bailiff, the clerk and the two armed marshals gasped in delighted indignation as a camera focused on a woman's vulva, where the doctor was inserting a speculum. A nurse, back to the camera, was bathing the woman's forehead with a towel. After a moment, blood flowed. The camera zoomed in on a blood clot, which Coulter identified as a dead baby.

After letting Justice Sessions and the rest of the all-male court lick their lips for a long moment, Coulter showed a video of the alley behind the clinic. A dark van was backed up to the clinic's rear door.

"We can't see who is coming out at this particular moment, but we do know that Dr. Herschel used this and other vehicles to whisk away illegals before ICE agents could demand their papers. Of course, once we spotted the ruse, we stopped the vans and arrested the occupants."

Here, the video showed Immigration & Customs Enforcement agents stopping several different vehicles. They pulled out women and children, cuffed them and thrust them into government cars. Dr. Herschel's lawyer directed a contemptuous smile at the prosecution table and made a point of writing an exceptionally long note. She whispered something to her own chief associate. The young man once again bit back a guffaw, earning yet another frown from Justice Sessions.

The final charge against the doctor claimed she'd helped spirit away the notorious immigration activist Sofia Hamer. Since appearing on the FBI's ten most wanted list, Hamer had been hidden in churches and attics by sympathizers across the nation. Every time the government seemed poised to make an arrest, it turned out they had the wrong information, or, worse, someone at the FBI or ICE had leaked the raid and given Hamer time to make her getaway.

Finally, thirteen months ago, they were sure they had cornered Hamer in a Chicago garden shop. The shop made a delivery of gladioli and day lilies to Dr. Herschel inside a long carton; Hamer, supposedly, lay underneath the flowers.

At the clinic, someone, perhaps the doctor, perhaps one of her staff, styled Hamer's hair to resemble the doctor's own, streaked it with white dye, put her in a lab coat and brazenly sent her outside.

"The agent detailed to follow the doctor had stepped away from his post for three minutes – even our dedicated ICE agents sometimes have a call from nature." The reporter noted laughter from Sessions and the other four judges.

"The clinic staff seemed to be watching our agent, because they used that window of time to send Hamer out; she drove off in Dr. Herschel's own Audi."

The Audi had been found in the meatpacking district; the doctor was in surgery all day and claimed to know nothing about Hamer. "Of course she knew about

Hamer: why else did she leave her Audi at the clinic instead of driving herself to the hospital?"

Ruth Lebeau cross-examined the agent to no avail: wasn't it true that Dr. Herschel often used a car service between the clinic and the hospital? Wasn't it true that she was often in the operating room for ten or even fifteen hours, so that she was too fatigued to drive herself at the end of surgery?

"You're arguing generalities," Justice Session rebuked Lebeau. "We're looking at a specific day and a particular crime."

At the end of the eighth day, the prosecution rested. "The government has irrefutable evidence that warrants that Dr. Herschel be stripped of her U.S. citizenship. However, we believe her crimes rise to the level of deliberate treason against the United States by refusing to acknowledge the power of the Government to pass the Keep American Safe act, and to enforce its provisions."

Coulter wiped his mouth with the red handkerchief he kept in his breast pocket for such moments and resumed his seat. Justice Sessions adjourned the court and said they would hear the defense in the morning. He and Melvin Coulter rode down the elevator together and were later seen yet again at the Potawatomi Club, laughing over their drinks – martini for the prosecutor, iced tea for the abstemious justice.

All during the final day of the prosecution's case, Coulter had been smirking with his juniors at the prosecution table, watching as Ruth Lebeau sent her own young team members out in flocks.

In the morning, it became clear that the defense was in trouble, and why: their key witnesses had disappeared. The detective V.I. Warshawski, who had gathered much of the defense's evidence, was in prison herself: she'd been arrested two days earlier, charged under the same sections of the Keep American Safe act as Dr. Herschel.

The court reporter thought Dr. Herschel was going to faint. Her dark, vivid face turned pale and waxy and she swayed in her seat. Ruth Lebeau, her attorney, asked if she needed a break.

"I require water," the doctor said.

Ruth Lebeau's chief associate produced a large thermos of hot water from his case and poured a cup for the doctor. Since the rest of her witnesses had been disappeared, Lebeau called the doctor to the stand.

As the doctor spoke, her vocal cords gradually regained their flexibility. The court reporter had strained to understand her at first, but after half an hour, the grating harshness left the doctor's voice. She spoke clearly, almost musically: the reporter realized it was a pleasure to listen to her after all the men she'd been recording during the prosecution phase. Too much bullying and swagger, none of this evenness, this effort to be clear that the doctor exhibited.

"I treat everyone who comes to my clinic," Dr. Herschel said. "I don't need to see a driver's license or a passport to diagnose measles or an ectopic pregnancy."

On cross-examination, Coulter demanded to know why she'd refused to treat the pregnant woman who'd been brought to her jail cell.

"I am curious about your knowledge of this woman," the doctor said. "Did you direct the guards to bring her to my cell?"

The members of the tribunal seemed to gasp, but Justice Sessions said, "You are on the stand, doctor. You don't get to ask questions."

The doctor bowed her head.

"You must answer the Attorney," Sessions said.

"The woman was not pregnant," Dr. Herschel said.

"You refused to examine her, so how can you possibly know this?" Coulter asked.

"How many pregnant women have you examined in your legal career, Mr. Coulter?" the doctor said. "Oh, yes, I must not ask you questions. But we will assume it is one woman, your wife, who produced two children with you. I have seen thousands. I know the difference between an abdomen with a fetus inside it, and a body with a pillow buckled to it. Perhaps you would have been fooled, but I was not."

"You can't know that!" Coulter snapped.

The doctor shrugged but remained silent.

"Have you nothing to say?" Sessions demanded.

Before Lebeau could jump to her feet to remind the court that Coulter had made a statement, not asked a question, the doctor said, "I have lived a long life. I have seen governments taken over by ravening weasels, I have watched them incite bored or ignorant or fearful mobs to violence. That you would bribe or coerce a woman to pretend a pregnancy does not surprise me, but it does sicken me."

Coulter sat down again. There was a moment of

silence and then Ruth Lebeau asked the prosecution to put up one of their videos of a couple of women being pulled from an SUV in handcuffs. She zoomed in on their faces and asked the doctor if she recognized them.

"Yes, they were patients, first in my clinic, and then, because the daughter had complications, I saw her in surgery at Beth Israel."

"And can you identify them, by name, I mean?" Lebeau asked.

"I can, but I will not. It is enough that these strange men can look at them and know they sought medical help, but I will not violate their privacy further by naming them."

"Did you know that the older woman was Justice Sessions housekeeper?" Lebeau asked.

The doctor's eyes widened: the court reporter, barely keeping back a gasp herself, thought the doctor hadn't known. "I did not know that, but I do not discriminate among those I treat."

"And did you know the daughter, whose abortion you performed, had been raped by the justice?"

At that, Sessions slammed his gavel and demanded an end to the proceedings. "The defense will rest. They cannot call independent witnesses to this calumny --"

"Yes, we cannot call your housekeeper, who looked after you for twenty-three years, because she was deported last week, was she not?" Lebeau said.

"That was a decision by Immigration & Customs, not by me. The court is adjourned for today. The tribunal will meet tomorrow to discuss a verdict."

The court reporter couldn't sleep that night. She was shocked by today's testimony. Abortion was evil, and the doctor was wicked to perform them. But Justice Sessions – when the black lady lawyer said he'd raped his housekeeper's daughter, he'd ended the trial. If he'd been innocent, surely he would have denied the accusation.

The court reporter had a high security clearance, which required her to sign papers promising never to speak to anyone about the proceedings she attended. She thought of her oath, she thought of the doctor, the presiding justice, the men licking their lips at the video of the naked woman's vagina.

At five in the morning, she got up and went down the street to her local drugstore. The clerk was yawning, barely awake, counting the seconds until her overnight shift would end. The reporter, her hands shaking, paid cash for a cheap phone. She made a call to the cousin who had helped get her the job with the federal courts.

In the morning, the tribunal met for less than an hour before summoning the prisoner. The court reporter could see that the doctor had probably not slept any more than she had herself. The doctor's walnut-colored skin was pale, her eyes a pair of black holes sunk deep in her face.

Justice Sessions said, "The court has voted four to one to find you guilty on all counts under the Keep America Safe Act. We debated stripping you of your citizenship and deporting you, but we are well aware that your native country, Austria, is prepared to make you an international heroine and martyr, and so we are sentencing you to natural life in a federal prison in the United States. The Federal Bureau of Prisons will inform your attorney when they have decided where to house you. For now, you will remain in Chicago in the care of the Metropolitan Correctional Center. Court is adjourned."

A marshal seized Dr. Herschel and marched her through the side door that led to the fenced in yard at the back of the building where prisoners were transferred into the buses that returned them to the various jails around town.

Her lawyer and the lawyer's chief associate walked with the doctor as far as the exit: they weren't permitted beyond the doorway. As she tried to thank the lawyer, the doctor seemed to stumble. Lebeau's young associate caught her as she fainted.

He pulled his thermos from his brief case and unscrewed the top. No one could agree what happened next, but one of the marshals thought the young lawyer poured a glass bottle labeled "sugar" into the thermos. Smoke billowed out. It covered the doctor, the lawyer, the marshal and spread through the fenced-in courtyard. The marshals pulled their weapons and began firing into the thick fog, but someone screamed: they'd hit the driver of the prison van, who'd been standing behind it waiting to lock the doctor inside. By the time the fog cleared, the prison van was gone.

Later that day, the van was discovered at Belmont Harbor on the Chicago shore of Lake Michigan. The Coast Guard began a search of all boats on the lake, but they didn't find the doctor, Lebeau's chief associate, or the federal marshal who'd handcuffed the doctor as she was taken from the courtroom. No one noticed that the court reporter had also disappeared.

Months went by; the Department of Justice kept close surveillance on anyone who might be in touch with the doctor, including the imprisoned V.I. Warshawski, who'd been the doctor's close friend for decades. They monitored the doctor's family members in Canada, her medical colleagues, even some of her high-profile patients. No one spoke of her. No one heard from her.

Time passed. Crops were rotting in the fields because the immigrants who used to harvest them were denied entry or had been deported from a safe America. Construction sites languished. The 117th Congress overturned the most stringent sections of the Keep America Safe Act, although the criminal penalties for performing abortions on U.S.-born women remained in place.

Somewhere along the way, V.I. Warshawski was released from prison. She, too, disappeared without a trace, despite the FBI's continued monitoring of her actions.

Every now and then, the FBI or ICE would follow up on a report of a small, black-eyed doctor performing miracle cures among indigenous Americans, or in Congo or Central America. She had a few assistants, who helped trace rapists or murderers or thieves in whatever village or jungle they found themselves, but by the time U.S. agents were dispatched across deserts and mountains, these legendary figures had moved on.

This story was written for the anthology, It Occurs to Me that I Am America, Jonathan Santlofer, ed, Touchstone Books, 2018. The fifty-two writers and artists who contributed work did so without pay so that all income from the book could support the American Civil Liberties Union. It is printed here with permission of Wm. Morrow.

Sara Paretsky revolutionized the mystery world in 1982 when she introduced V.I. Warshawski in **Indemnity Only.** By creating a detective with the grit and smarts to take on the mean streets, Paretsky challenged a genre in which women historically were vamps or victims. V.I. struck a chord with readers and critics; Indemnity Only was followed by twenty more V.I. novels. Her voice and her world remain vital to readers; the *New York Times* calls V.I., "a proper hero for these times," adding, "to us, V.I. is perfect."

While Paretsky's fiction changed the narrative about women, her work also opened doors for other writers. In 1986 she created Sisters in Crime, a worldwide organization to advocate for women crime writers, which earned her Ms. Magazine's 1987 Woman of the Year award. More accolades followed: the British Crime Writers awarded her the Cartier Diamond Dagger for lifetime achievement; Blacklist won the Gold Dagger from the British Crime Writers for best novel of 2004, and she has received the honorary degree of Doctor of Letters from a number of universities.

Called "passionate" and "electrifying," V.I. reflects her creator's own passion for social justice. After chairing the school's first Commission on the Status of Women as a Kansas University undergraduate, Paretsky worked as a community organizer on Chicago's South

Side during the turbulent race riots of 1966. Since then, Paretsky's volunteer work has included advocating for healthcare for the mentally ill homeless; mentoring teens in Chicago's most troubled schools, and working for reproductive rights. Through her Sara & Two C-Dogs foundation, she also helps build STEM and arts programs for young people.

The actress Kathleen Turner played V.I. Warshawski in the movie of that name. Paretsky's work is celebrated in Pamela Beere Briggs's documentary, **Women of Mystery**. Today Sara Paretsky's books are published in 30 countries.

Paretsky detailed her journey from Kansas farm-girl to *New York Times* bestseller in her 2007 memoir, **Writing in an Age of Silence**, which was a National Book Critics Circle Award finalist. In addition, Paretsky has written two stand-alone novels, **Ghost Country**, and **Bleeding Kansas**, set in the part of rural Kansas where Paretsky grew up. She has published several short story collections, most recently **Love & Other Crimes**, and has edited numerous other anthologies.

Like her fictional detective, Paretsky has an adored Golden Retriever. Like alto Warshawski, soprano Paretsky doesn't work hard enough at her vocal exercises, but the two women share a love for espresso and rich Italian reds.

All proceeds from this book will be donated to
organizations supporting reproductive heath care.